OXFORD
UNIVERSITY PRESS

Great Clarendon Street, Oxford OX2 6DP

Oxford University Press is a department of the University of Oxford.
It furthers the University's objective of excellence in research, scholarship,
and education by publishing worldwide in

Oxford New York

Athens Auckland Bangkok Bogotá Buenos Aires Calcutta
Cape Town Chennai Dar es Salaam Delhi Florence Hong Kong Istanbul
Karachi Kuala Lumpur Madrid Melbourne Mexico City Mumbai
Nairobi Paris São Paulo Singapore Taipei Tokyo Toronto Warsaw

with associated companies in Berlin Ibadan

Oxford is a registered trade mark of Oxford University Press
in the UK and in certain other countries

British Library Cataloguing in Publication Data available

ISBN 0-19-279052-8 (hardback)
ISBN 0-19-272409-6 (paperback)

1 3 5 7 9 10 8 6 4 2

Typeset by Danny McBride Graphic Design
Printed and bound in Malaysia

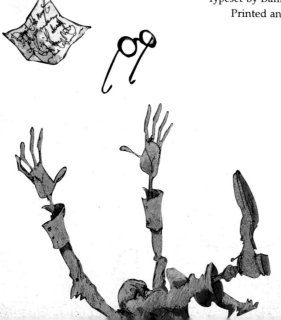

Dr Jekyll and Mr Hyde

Adapted and Illustrated by

Chris Mould

OXFORD
UNIVERSITY PRESS

The Door

Mr Utterson was a lawyer. Cold, and hardened through his experience, yet he was lovable. One of his friends was Mr Richard Enfield. Although they seldom spoke and found little in common on their Sunday walks, they enjoyed these outings.

By chance, one of these rambles led them down a street in a busy quarter of London. A sinister looking building butted outward into the street. Two storeys high and showing no window, there was but one door on the lower floor. Mr Enfield pointed with his cane. 'Did you ever see that door before?' he questioned. 'For it brings to mind a very strange tale.'

'I was returning home early one morning,' began Mr Enfield. 'I spied two figures. The first, a young girl, running fast; the second, a small man, lurching along. At the corner they collided and the man, unconcerned, trampled over the girl. I collared him and returned to find the girl surrounded by her family. They demanded a hundred pounds to avoid a scene. The man agreed calmly. But where do you think he went to get the money? That very door, sir.'

'Do you know the name of this man?' asked Utterson.

'It's Mr Edward Hyde,' replied Enfield. 'A detestable man.'

'That door leads to the house of my friend Dr Jekyll,' whispered Mr Utterson uneasily.

In Search of Mr Hyde

That evening Mr Utterson reached home in troubled spirits. From his safe he took Dr Jekyll's will: in the case of the death of Henry Jekyll all his possessions were to pass to his friend Edward Hyde; in the case of his disappearance, Hyde should step into Jekyll's place. This document troubled him. Who was Hyde and what was the reason for the strange will?

Mr Utterson sought out his friend Dr Lanyon. 'I suppose we must be the two oldest friends that Henry Jekyll has,' began Mr Utterson.

'Quite so,' agreed Dr Lanyon. 'Though I seldom see him now.' (They had disagreed over scientific matters and had drifted apart.)

'Did you ever come across a friend of his named Hyde?' enquired Utterson.

'No,' was his reply.

That night Utterson tossed and turned in his bed. Mr Enfield's tale unfolded in his head, over and over. The light from a thousand street lamps lit his nightmare. He tried to see Hyde's face but saw only the dark creatures of his imagination.

From that time onward Utterson began to haunt the doorway, morning, noon, and night, hoping to catch sight of Edward Hyde.

At last his patience was rewarded. On a frosty night a small odd looking man approached as Utterson hid in the shadows. He drew a key from his pocket. Utterson stepped out. 'Mr Hyde, I think.'

Hyde recoiled in horror. 'That is my name. What do you want?'

'I am a friend of Dr Jekyll, perhaps you will admit me?'

'He is not at home now. How did you know me?'

'You fit your description. We have friends in common. Henry Jekyll is one.'

'He never described me to you!' cried Hyde, angered. Then he lowered his tone. 'Perhaps it is as well we have met.' And he gave the lawyer his address.

The next moment Hyde unlocked the door and disappeared into the house.

Mr Utterson made his way to the front door. Poole, the butler, admitted him. 'I will see if Dr Jekyll is at home, sir.' The doctor was out.

'I saw Mr Hyde enter. Is that right when Dr Jekyll is out?' quizzed Utterson.

'Yes, sir,' insisted Poole. 'He is to have access at all times. He comes and goes by the laboratory.'

Utterson left, turning the will over in his mind. If Hyde knows the contents of the will he may grow impatient to inherit, he thought.

A fortnight later Mr Utterson was dining at Dr Jekyll's. After dinner the two sat together by the fire.

'I've been wanting to speak to you,' said Utterson. 'It's about your will.'

'I know you never approved,' Jekyll said uneasily.

'Well, I approve even less now that I have seen your Mr Hyde.'

Jekyll's face grew pale. 'I wish to hear no more,' he said.

'I have heard a terrible story concerning him,' continued Utterson.

'My position is strange,' explained Jekyll. 'The moment I choose I can be rid of Hyde. I know you've seen him, but if you knew everything you would stand by my will. You must promise.'

And he did so, but with a heavy heart.

The Carew Murder

It was almost a year later when a crime startled the whole of London. A maidservant, living alone, had gone to bed around eleven. Her window overlooked a winding lane. She saw an elderly gentleman walking along and a smaller man heading in his direction.

She recognized the latter as Mr Hyde, who visited her master, Dr Jekyll. The elderly man began a conversation but Hyde suddenly attacked him for no reason, and clubbed him to the ground. At this the maid fainted.

At two o'clock she came to and called for the police. The murderer was long gone but there lay the body and half of the walking stick that was used to batter him. The following morning Mr Utterson identified the body as that of Sir Danvers Carew. The police inspector listened to the maid's story and Mr Utterson pondered over the broken stick. There was no doubt: it was one he had presented to Dr Jekyll himself. Immediately they went to the address of Mr Hyde.

The inspector insisted on searching the house and there, behind the door in Hyde's room, lay the missing half of the broken stick. Proof that Hyde was their man.

When they reached the door a woman answered. 'Yes, this is the home of Mr Hyde, but he is not here, sir. He came in late last night but went out again within the hour.'

The Letter

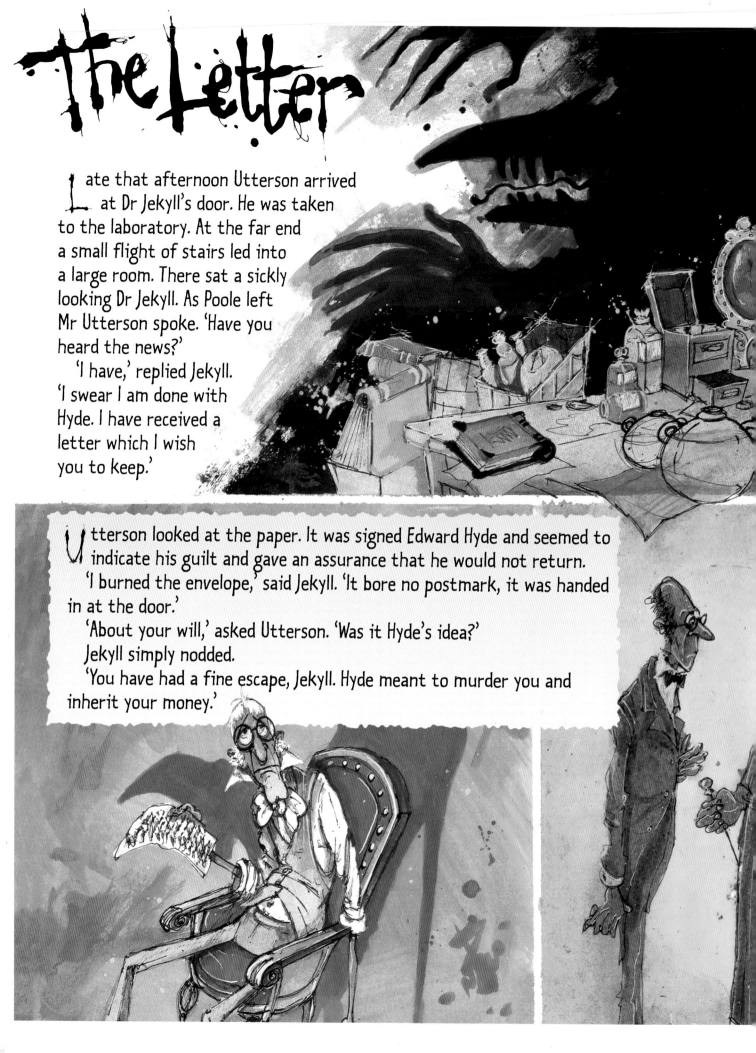

Late that afternoon Utterson arrived at Dr Jekyll's door. He was taken to the laboratory. At the far end a small flight of stairs led into a large room. There sat a sickly looking Dr Jekyll. As Poole left Mr Utterson spoke. 'Have you heard the news?'

'I have,' replied Jekyll. 'I swear I am done with Hyde. I have received a letter which I wish you to keep.'

Utterson looked at the paper. It was signed Edward Hyde and seemed to indicate his guilt and gave an assurance that he would not return.

'I burned the envelope,' said Jekyll. 'It bore no postmark, it was handed in at the door.'

'About your will,' asked Utterson. 'Was it Hyde's idea?'

Jekyll simply nodded.

'You have had a fine escape, Jekyll. Hyde meant to murder you and inherit your money.'

On his way out Utterson questioned Poole about the letter. 'I'm sorry, sir. I know nothing about a letter,' he claimed. Utterson left in confusion. Someone was hiding something.

Back at home Utterson confided in his clerk, Mr Guest, a handwriting expert. 'I have a letter here from the murderer in the Carew case. Would you take a look?'

'An odd hand indeed, sir,' he said. And then, taking a dinner invitation from Dr Jekyll, he placed the two side by side.

'Why do you compare them?' asked Utterson.

'Well, sir, there is a great resemblance, only Mr Hyde's writing is strangely sloped.'

'We must not speak of this,' insisted Utterson as he put the letter into his safe.

His heart beat faster. Henry Jekyll forging for a murderer, he thought, and the blood ran cold in his veins.

As time passed great rewards were offered, but it appeared that Hyde had disappeared for good. Much was unearthed of his callousness, his violent nature, but as to his whereabouts, not a whisper.

Now that the evil influence had gone, Dr Jekyll became himself again.

In January, Utterson, Lanyon, and Jekyll rekindled their friendship but suddenly, Jekyll confined himself to the house once more. Shortly after this Utterson visited Dr Lanyon and was alarmed to find him very ill. He declared that he had suffered a terrible shock and was a doomed man.

'It appears that Jekyll is also ill!' exclaimed Utterson.

'I am quite done with Jekyll. I wish to hear no more of him.'

On Utterson's return home he penned a letter to Jekyll. Why was he excluded from the house? What had caused the terrible rift with Lanyon? The next day brought a mysterious reply.

From now on I must lead a life of extreme seclusion, Jekyll wrote. Do not doubt my friendship, even if my door is shut to you.

Utterson was left amazed. Hyde had gone, and the doctor had returned to his old life, but in view of Lanyon's present state, something lay unanswered.

Shortly after, Dr Lanyon died.

Following the funeral, Utterson sat at home alone. He held a letter from Lanyon. 'For the hands of J. G. Utterson alone and in the case of his predecease to be destroyed unread.' Within was a further enclosure. 'Not to be opened until the death or disappearance of Dr Henry Jekyll.' What could this mean?

The following Sunday, by chance, Mr Utterson and Mr Enfield passed the door once again.

'Well, Utterson, we shall see no more of Mr Hyde.'

'I hope not,' replied Utterson. 'To tell you the truth I am quite worried about poor Jekyll. I feel the presence of a friend would do him good.' And they stepped into the court.

One of the windows was open. Utterson could see Jekyll.
'Jekyll, I trust you are better.'
'No, I am very low, Utterson.'
'Then you must walk with us, sir.'
'No, I cannot, but it is good to see you.'

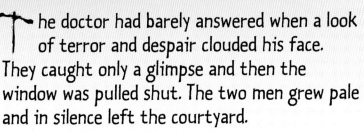

The doctor had barely answered when a look of terror and despair clouded his face. They caught only a glimpse and then the window was pulled shut. The two men grew pale and in silence left the courtyard.

The Last Night

Mr Utterson was surprised to receive a visit from Poole one evening.

'There is something wrong, Mr Utterson. Please come to the house and see for yourself. There has been foul play.'

When they reached the house Poole knocked at Jekyll's door and informed him that Mr Utterson was there.

'Tell him I cannot see him,' replied Jekyll.

'His voice, Mr Utterson, did you notice a difference?' gasped Poole. 'Two or three times a day I have gone to the chemist for medicine, but he complained it was not pure. When I appeared he ran back into his room. And he was wearing a mask.'

'Maybe he has been gripped by an illness that has changed him, hence the mask and his voice.'

'But, sir, he was short. My master is tall and finely built.'

'I believe poor Henry has been killed by Mr Hyde,' said Mr Utterson. 'Let us break down the door.'

They did so. There, on the floor, lay the body of Edward Hyde, dead by his own hand. There was no trace of Henry Jekyll.

On the desk there were papers. One was Jekyll's will, re-drawn in favour of Utterson. The second was a note from Jekyll. 'The end is near for me. Go and read Lanyon's letter. Then read my confession.'

Dr Lanyon's Story

Utterson held Dr Lanyon's letter which was only to be opened upon the death or disappearance of Henry Jekyll. He began to read:

On the 9th January I received a letter from Dr Jekyll. This is how the letter began:

Dear Lanyon,
Although we have differed on scientific matters my affection for you remains unbroken.
Now I ask of you a great favour.

The letter continued in its instructions. I was to go to Jekyll's house that night where Poole would meet me. We should take out the drawer of his desk by force. I should then return with it to Cavendish Square. A man would appear at midnight to collect.

Serve me my dear Lanyon and save your friend. H. J.

I felt sure my colleague was insane, yet I felt bound to do as he asked. I examined the drawer. It was filled with powders, and a container of liquid. The knocker sounded. A small, ugly man crouched there wearing clothes which were too large for him. He sprang to the drawer and drank a mixture he concocted. Suddenly he seemed to be changing. His features altered. I screamed in terror. There was the man I knew as Henry Jekyll, but the creature who had crept into my house had been Edward Hyde, the murderer.

Hastie Lanyon

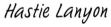

How could Utterson ever have imagined the truth? Jekyll and Hyde were one and the same person. It was quite inconceivable, yet it answered every question. Utterson turned to Dr Jekyll's statement.

Dr Jekyll's Story

I was born into a large fortune with every hope of a distinguished future. My worst fault was a love for life's pleasures which was ill matched with my desire for public respect. I had therefore already created two lives for myself. I was equally at ease as the pleasure-seeking rake as I was as the gentlemanly doctor. I came to believe that a man is two people, not one.

I fantasized about the possibility of being able to separate myself. Through my scientific study I was one night to realize just that. I watched my ingredients boil and smoke in the glass.
And then I drank . . .

I stole through the house as a different person, a stranger. Then I looked in my mirror and saw for the first time, Edward Hyde. I saw evil in that face yet I felt a leap of welcome. I returned to my laboratory and drank the mixture once more. Instantly I was Jekyll again. My experiment was complete and I could lead a double life.

I suffered pangs . . . a grinding in my bones and a horror of the spirit.
Then it subsided. I felt younger, brighter, happier and a wickedness boiled inside me.

I took and furnished the house in Soho. At the same time I announced to my servants that a Mr Hyde was to have access to the house at any time and to obey him as they would me. Next I drew up the will to cover myself in the event of any mishap.

Whilst in the guise of Hyde, the conscience of Jekyll slumbered. Hyde was guilty, not Jekyll, of the trampling of a poor child.

Before the murder of Carew I had been out late one night. When I awoke I saw I had the hands of Hyde. I rushed to the mirror. I had gone to bed as Jekyll and woken as Hyde. How could this be? I had not taken the drug. I feared this thing had gripped me harder than I liked and so I resolved not to take the drug for two months.

But in a moment of weakness I swallowed the potion once more and Mr Hyde, like a caged animal, came surging out.

It was on this night that I encountered Carew whom I knocked to the ground with my stick. But as the mist cleared I realized the atrocity should not be laid at the feet of Dr Jekyll. I made haste to Soho and removed all evidence of a link between the two. I broke the key to the door but in my panic I forgot the broken stick. Daylight brought the news of a witness who had identified Mr Hyde.

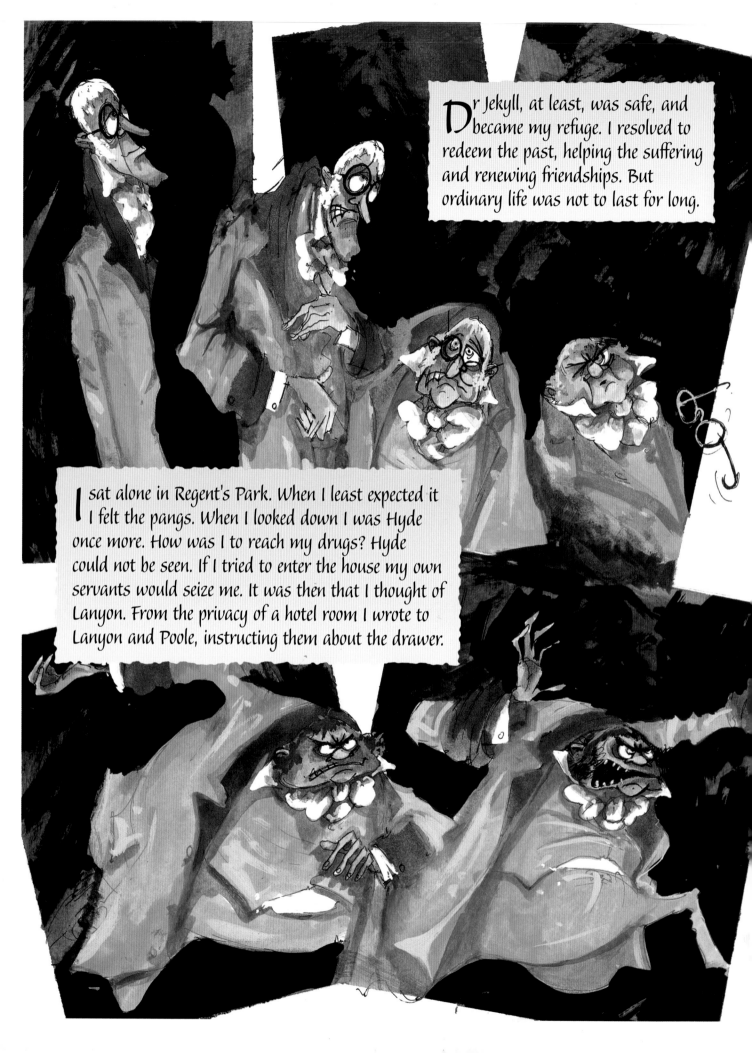

Dr Jekyll, at least, was safe, and became my refuge. I resolved to redeem the past, helping the suffering and renewing friendships. But ordinary life was not to last for long.

I sat alone in Regent's Park. When I least expected it I felt the pangs. When I looked down I was Hyde once more. How was I to reach my drugs? Hyde could not be seen. If I tried to enter the house my own servants would seize me. It was then that I thought of Lanyon. From the privacy of a hotel room I wrote to Lanyon and Poole, instructing them about the drawer.

Upon reaching Lanyon, Hyde transformed himself before his eyes. This proved too much for Lanyon. After I arrived home I realized I was not safe anywhere. I could transform at any moment. I left notes for Poole to fetch me chemicals but they no longer worked.

I am finishing this statement under the last of my potions. This is the last time I will see my own face in the glass. If Hyde finds this statement he will destroy it. Will Hyde die on the gallows or have the courage to finish himself off? I care not as I lay down my pen and bring the life of that unhappy Henry Jekyll to an end.